MW00945746

Strawberry Rose

D. D. Glover

Illustrated by
Signe Berglind Hill

Dream
Garden

This is a work of fiction. All of the characters, names, incidents, organizations, and dialogue in this book are either products of the author's imagination or are used fictitiously.

Cover art and illustrations by Signe Berglind Hill. Edited by C. M. Schmidt and. S. C. Moore.

978-1-938281-81-5   (hardback)
978-1-938281-82-2   (paperback)
978-1-938281-83-9   (e-book)

Library of Congress Control Number: 2020922278

Published 2020, Dream Garden Publications, an imprint of Gazebo Gardens Publishing, LLC.
www.GazeboGardensPublishing.com

Printed in the United States of America.

To my grandchildren.

Strawberry Rose is inspired by
the real-life adventures of the author
during her summer visits as a child
to her grandparents' cabin at the lake.

Table of Contents

CHAPTER ONE

Strawberry Picking

It was raining. The drops mixed with the dust on the sleeping porch screen, filling the air with a muddy scent. It was night, so Rose couldn't see the waves crashing on the lakeshore, but she could hear them.

The top bunk bed creaked as Rose moved deeper under the covers and snuggled into the rough sheets covered by an old wool blanket. She didn't feel cold but was comforting herself with the weight of the heavy folds of cloth.

Rose wasn't sure if she could sleep with her mixed feelings of excitement and nerves. She was spending the summer with her grandparents at their cabin on the lake, and this was the first time she was going to be away from home, without her parents, for this long. But, she was nine years old—almost ten—and Rose thought she was old enough to be brave.

Her grandparents' dog, Goose, was asleep on a worn-out quilt next to the lower bunk. He was a black Labrador mix, and it was hard to see him in the dark. Rose could hear him breathing. She was glad that his bed was also on the sleeping porch.

The rain had stopped. Rose finally fell asleep to the low croak of the bullfrogs singing where the creek met the lakeshore.

The morning sun suddenly shone brightly into the screened sleeping porch. Rose slowly opened her eyes. She could see the lake from her top bunk, and it was as smooth as glass.

There was no sign of last night's storm, except for the smell of damp pine that was quickly drying out in the sunshine. Goose had already left his spot next to the bottom bunk, and Rose could smell bacon cooking.

She had arrived yesterday with just a backpack and a small duffel bag. Rose remembered feeling sad to leave home as she said goodbye to her parents, but she was also bubbling with anticipation for a fun-filled summer.

When her grandfather picked her up in the city, he tossed both of her bags into the back of his truck and commented on how light her luggage was. Her grandfather didn't say much more, but Rose was content to just look out the window as they drove along.

The scenery through the truck window began to change as rolling fields were replaced by bigger trees.

After traveling what seemed like forever to Rose, but was really only half a day, they turned around a bend.

Rose shouted out excitedly, "Grandpa, I see the lake!"

It shimmered in the sunlight, and the bright blue color of the water matched the sky.

They drove around another corner and onto a gravel driveway. It led to her grandparents' dark green cabin overlooking the lake. It looked just like Rose remembered from when she'd visited with her parents last summer.

The wooden cabin was surrounded by fruit trees and so many giant pine trees that Rose lost count. It had a brown roof, with the windows trimmed in white, and a path out front that went down the bluff to the lake and the dock. There was a screened porch across the entire lakefront-facing side, which was Rose's favorite place because in the corner was her creaky but sturdy bunk bed.

Sitting up in that very bed, Rose realized she was hungry. She remembered that after the long, dusty, and bumpy drive in the truck, she hadn't eaten much dinner. Rose grabbed some clothes from her duffel bag, quickly got dressed, and went out to find that bacon.

Rose's grandmother was in the kitchen moving between the stove and the sink, smiling and chatting away. She talked quickly, but Rose didn't mind—she liked hearing her grandmother's happy voice.

Grandma was dressed in a cream colored blouse, and over it was a pretty bright green apron that had a ruffle on the bottom edge. She was wearing brown pants with matching flat shoes that Rose thought looked nice. Her silver hair was tidy and put up with a clip.

Often, Grandma had mentioned that she had red hair when she was a girl, and it was the color of sunshine—just like Rose's. That made her granddaughter feel special.

"Did you sleep well, Rose?"

Rose nodded slightly and smiled. "I love sleeping on the screened porch."

"I'm so glad, dear," Grandma responded. "Here is your breakfast. Do you want some jam for your toast? I hope you like scrambled eggs. After you eat, I'll send you out to pick strawberries. Grandpa is already outside with Goose. He'll show you the garden, and you may find some wild strawberries too. It's a beautiful day."

Rose nodded again and silently finished eating. Then, she clutched the strawberry-picking bucket Grandma had handed to her, thanked Grandma for breakfast, and went out the kitchen door. It closed softly behind her.

It was beautiful outside. The air was still, and the lake sparkled. Rose spotted an eagle high up in a tall, scraggly pine. The eagle spread its wings and swooped down to what looked like a glimmer on the lake's surface. The big bird grabbed a fish in its talons and soared away from the bay.

There was a noise behind her. Rose quickly turned around before Goose almost toppled her over in excitement. He wagged his whole body, not just his tail. He calmed down enough to lead Rose to where Grandpa was working in the garden.

"Hi, sleepyhead!" her grandfather called out. "I know how much you like strawberries, and there are plenty of ripe ones." He nodded toward an area of the garden full of bushy plants.

Rose took her bucket and leaned over a strawberry plant while pushing aside the green leaves. There were small green berries, white ones, and white strawberries just turning red. She spotted the fully red ripe ones and went to work filling her bucket to the brim. Goose took an interest in what she was doing at first. But then he sat down near where Grandpa was tending to his vegetables.

Grandpa was wearing a braided straw hat with a big brim to shade his face from the sun. He would take it off and wipe his ragged face with a red handkerchief when he got too hot. His silver hair was wild and messy, and Rose liked it that way. He was big and very tall but was always so careful with his tiny plants. Rose thought it was fun to work with him in the garden.

Rose picked as many as she could then carried the bucket of strawberries back to the house. Goose followed her.

In the kitchen, her grandmother admired the full bucket. "You did a nice job, Rose. Look at all those strawberries!"

Grandpa came into the kitchen and winked at Rose. Goose wagged his tail.

The table was already set with a big pile of sandwiches. Grandma added a large bowl of rinsed strawberries to the meal, and they ate them for dessert.

After lunch, Rose washed and dried the dishes. Grandpa had fallen asleep while reading a book in his old recliner chair. Grandma was sitting comfortably on the couch surrounded by a stack of books, some knitting supplies, and a basket of items needing mending.

While her grandparents were resting, Rose went outside with Goose. She carried a small bucket in case she found wild strawberries, which were smaller than the ones in the garden but fun to find.

Strawberries are my favorite fruit,"

Rose told Goose.

He wagged his tail as if he agreed.

Rose walked behind the house and along the old orchard path. After a short distance, the path ended at a meadow. There were wild strawberry plants everywhere. Rose knelt down and started picking the tiny, red, fragrant berries. She heard a sound behind her, and at first, she thought it was Goose.

When Rose turned around, she saw a girl standing there with one hand on her petite hip. She was taller than Rose but a little thinner. She wore flowers in her windswept brown hair. Rose noticed that the girl's bright purple shirt was embroidered with pretty yellow flowers.

"Hi!" the girl said. Her dark brown eyes lit up as she smiled. "You must be Rose. Around here, people call me Buttercup."

Goose bounded up to the new arrival and wagged his tail rapidly. Rose almost knocked over her strawberry bucket as she stood up to greet Buttercup.

"Hi," Rose answered shyly.

Buttercup prattled on, "I'm visiting my aunt in the bay, and she said that you were staying here for the summer and I should come and see if you wanted to hang out together."

"Sure," said Rose. "Grandma mentioned something about a girl around my age in the bay, but I think her name was Trudy."

The girl crinkled her freckled nose and said, "That name is only for town. Buttercup is my lake name. You need a summer name too! How about Strawberry Rose? You obviously like strawberries, and you do have that pretty red hair."

Rose looked down at her hair that she'd quickly put in braids that morning. It shined bright red in the sunlight. She nodded and then replied, "That would be fun. Strawberry Rose it is."

A deer wandered into the meadow, then another one. Goose ran after them.

Strawberry Rose called out, "Goose, you get back here! Leave those poor deer alone."

The dog turned around reluctantly and moseyed his way back to the girls, sniffing at mysterious things along the way.

Buttercup smiled and said, "Goose is an unusual name for a dog."

Strawberry Rose replied, "I was here with my mother when my grandparents got him as a puppy. I told them he was as silly as a goose, and the name stuck."

"At least he doesn't honk," Buttercup added.

Strawberry Rose nodded, and they both laughed.

Buttercup said she had to get back to her aunt's home in the bay, but they agreed to meet up at the lakeshore soon.

The two girls walked down the path together for a bit before separating to head home after saying their goodbyes.

That night, even with the light of a full moon streaming into the screened porch, Strawberry Rose fell asleep much faster. Goose did too.

CHAPTER TWO

Driftwood Beach

Strawberry Rose awoke with a sore throat and a fever, so it was a number of days before she could go to the lakeshore. Her grandmother kept her fully supplied with soup, things to drink, and lots of books to read.

She admired a pretty white and yellow daisy in a small glass vase on the table next to her bed. Every morning, a flower would mysteriously appear by the kitchen door, and her grandmother would bring it to her. Sometimes, the mystery flowers were a bunch of purple vetch flowers—and sometimes, golden buttercups. Once, it was a pink wild rose. But today, the surprise was a daisy.

Strawberry Rose was pretty sure she knew who was doing it.

She rested, and before too long, the fever broke, and she was feeling much better. So much so, that one afternoon, she asked her grandmother if she could go get the mail.

The mailboat came every day except Sunday. The shiny aluminum boat had a cover to keep the mailman and the packages protected from the sun, wind, and rain. They had the same mailboat delivery person every summer. His name was Clancy. Strawberry Rose didn't know if that was his first name or his last name. He always had a big, friendly grin.

Clancy carefully maneuvered his boat to the end of the dock where there was a mailbox on a pole that swiveled. There was also a container tied to the dock that could hold bigger packages.

Strawberry Rose waited until Clancy put the mail in the box and backed the boat away from the dock. He waved to her, and she waved back. Then, she turned the mailbox to be able to remove the mail. There were letters wrapped in a rubber band, but no packages.

As she started back to the house, she heard a familiar voice coming from a canoe that was approaching the dock.

"HI LO MINI MINI KA KA UM CHA CHA E WA WA!" Buttercup called out. "That's a canoe greeting."

Strawberry Rose answered, "EPTA MINIKA ONIKA ZONIKA BOOM DE YADA YOO HOO."

Buttercup almost fell out of her canoe and exclaimed, "How did you know that?"

"My mom taught me, and she learned it from growing up out here at the lake. Did you know there's one more response?"

Both girls yelled out, "FUNGI MUNGI CHICKEE I O," and then they giggled.

Buttercup said, "I'm so glad that you are feeling better!"

"Thank you, and thank you for the flowers."

Buttercup just grinned.

Goose ran past Strawberry Rose on the dock, almost knocking her over. He ran to the end and barked at Buttercup in her canoe, and then he picked up a stick on the dock. No one was making a move to throw it in the water for him, so he dropped it into the lake himself.

Goose looked a little guilty—as if there was a rule that dogs were not supposed to throw sticks for themselves. He barked at it and paced along the edge of the dock. Then he jumped in after the stick, splashing Buttercup in her canoe as he entered the water.

Goose grabbed the stick in his mouth, and as he turned, his tail slapped the water. He swam toward shore with all four legs paddling powerfully. Once Goose was on land, he dropped the stick and shook a fountain of spray off his black fur.

The girls laughed again, this time at the silly dog.

Strawberry Rose waved goodbye and headed back up the hill to give her grandparents the mail. She promised Buttercup that as soon as she was fully recovered and the lake warmed up a bit more, she would be back to swim.

Two black crows were arguing with each other just outside the screened porch when Strawberry Rose climbed out of bed. Clean clothes were folded neatly on the bottom bunk. Grandma had been busy this morning!

Last night, her grandfather had carried a small wooden dresser from another room and had placed it at the foot of the bunk bed. Strawberry Rose emptied her backpack contents and put the folded stack and the clothes from her duffel into the drawers.

Her clothes were mostly in her favorite colors of purple, blue, and pink. She placed her sparkly shirt with many colors carefully on top of the pile. Her mother had given it to her, and Strawberry Rose liked it a lot.

The bottom drawer already had things in it. She found playing cards, puzzles, crayons, markers, envelopes, paper, pens, and pencils. She found two other things that she put into her empty backpack.

Strawberry Rose had a soft blue sweatshirt, and she decided to put that in her pack as well. She left the backpack on the lower bunk and went to the kitchen to have breakfast.

She ate a bowl of cereal with sweet, sliced, fresh strawberries and then helped her grandmother wash the dishes. This time, Strawberry Rose washed, and Grandma dried the utensils, plates, cups, and bowls.

Strawberry Rose liked playing with the warm suds in the soapy water, but she worked fast so she could go outside. She had a surprise for Buttercup and wanted to meet her at the lakeshore.

It was already quite warm when Strawberry Rose, wearing her backpack, arrived at the beach. Goose led the way until he bounded off after a rabbit. He came back after a few minutes, fortunately unsuccessful in his bunny hunt.

Buttercup was already at the shore, walking along the water's edge. She was wearing a necklace woven from daisies.

"Hi, Strawberry Rose and Goose!" she gleefully called out. "I'm looking for pretty rocks. There are some cool ones like these." Buttercup held out her hand, showing bits and pieces of rocks. "These weird shaped ones are basalt, and these are quartz. I found an arrowhead here earlier this summer, and an old penny. I think it was 1902."

"Very cool," said Strawberry Rose. "Grandma told me that that long ago, the Native Americans had a winter camp in our bay. And later, there was a post office and store. Steamships would pull up to a dock and bring supplies."

"And I heard that a steamship sank in the lake once," remarked Buttercup.

"Yes, I heard that too."

The girls gazed out over the bay. The wind had picked up, and while the waves were rolling slowly in the bay, there were whitecaps out in the middle of the lake. When the waves were tipped in white, they knew it was windy and dangerous on the water.

Strawberry Rose continued, "I have an idea. Would you like to come with me to Driftwood Beach?"

"Sure," Buttercup said excitedly.

The two girls and Goose walked along the shore toward the creek. It wasn't something that would be difficult to wade across this time of year, but they crossed using the bridge anyway. A long time ago, someone built a small wooden bridge to span the creek, and it was still sturdy.

Halfway across, the girls stopped to look through the railing to watch the water slowly flow to the lake. The bridge wasn't very high. They could even touch the surface of the water with a long stick if they wanted to.

Strawberry Rose remembered her grandmother talk about how in the spring, the creek could rise as a raging river filled with icy cold snowmelt. Now, it wasn't very full or fast. She figured that as summer went along, it would dry to a trickle of water.

Three houses past the bridge, Buttercup ran into her aunt's house to tell her where they were going. Goose stayed with Strawberry Rose, and the dog eyed the geese that were keeping a safe distance from him.

As they both waited, Strawberry Rose looked along the shore for any unusual rocks. Nothing caught her attention, except for a small piece of weathered glass that had washed up on the beach. It had rounded edges so they weren't sharp. The glass was a pretty green color, and she put it in her pocket.

Buttercup ran from the house toward Strawberry Rose, with her backpack over her arm. She breathlessly called out, "Auntie packed us sandwiches and apples and filled us both water bottles. She had extra. She put in a treat for Goose too."

Goose looked up from whatever he was sniffing when he heard his name mentioned, and he wagged his tail.

"That's so nice. Be sure to thank her

later," Strawberry Rose replied.

Goose kept wagging his tail.

Strawberry Rose added, "See, Goose says thank you too."

The girls laughed. They were still giggling as they walked along the shore toward the edge of the bay.

There was a huge rock there that had weathered through the years, so it was full of cracks and broken stones. There was a narrow path that the girls and Goose used to scramble to the top.

Once there, they stopped to check out the view. The sky was big and blue with only a few clouds. The beach ahead was filled with driftwood. There were washed up tree trunks, branches, and other things. The wood had been bleached a light gray by the sun.

It was windy on the top of the rock, so Strawberry Rose pulled out her sweatshirt from her pack and put it on. Buttercup did the same with a sweater that was in her backpack.

"You're lucky, Goose—you have fur," Buttercup remarked.

Goose answered in agreement with a woof.

They carefully climbed down the path and started exploring the beach.

They looked at all the interesting pieces of gnarled wood. Strawberry Rose found two especially nice long flat pieces and put them on top of her pack.

Soon, even Goose was tired, so they sat on a big log and ate lunch. Goose's treat was a bone, and he happily chomped away.

The wind calmed down as they finished their sandwiches and most of their apples. Goose was happy to eat the apple cores.

Strawberry Rose picked up the two pieces of driftwood and pulled out the two other things she had put in her pack that morning. They were a package of elbow macaroni and some white glue.

"What are those for?" asked Buttercup.

"Here, let me show you," said Strawberry Rose. "We'll use the macaroni to spell our special lake names and glue it on the wood."

"That's cool," remarked Buttercup.

They spent the next half hour or so gluing the dried pasta on the driftwood while Goose fell asleep curled up in the sand. When they were done, they had their wood spellings, B U T T E R C U P on one board and S T R A W B E R R Y R O S E on the other. The sun quickly dried the glue, and they carefully held their signs as they walked back.

When they arrived at her aunt's house, Buttercup was still holding her driftwood sign in front of her. Before heading toward the door, she exclaimed, "This has been the best day ever!"

Strawberry Rose nodded in agreement and waved goodbye. She and Goose then walked slowly back to her grandparents' house

CHAPTER THREE

The Surprise

It was the hottest morning since Strawberry Rose arrived at the lake. As she jumped off the end of the dock, the cold water surrounded her, and it felt silky. She stayed underwater for a second just to feel the weightlessness and then came up for air.

Goose was barking at Strawberry Rose and looking nervously at Grandma sitting in a chair, under an umbrella, on the dock. Grandma didn't look concerned, so the dog lay down, but he watched Strawberry Rose intently.

Grandpa was working on something on his fishing boat that was tied to one side of the dock. Every once in a while,

Grandma would go over to join him to help. Strawberry Rose liked listening to them work and laugh together.

Soon, Buttercup paddled her canoe over and called out the greeting. She joined Strawberry Rose in swimming and splashing, and then they climbed out of the water.

The girls dried off by lying in the sun on a towel on the dock, and then they jumped into the water—again and again. Each time anyone jumped in the lake, Goose would go to the end of the dock and bark until he could see they were fine.

Grandma had packed a picnic lunch, so they soon stopped to eat. After enjoying their meal, they played on the beach for a while and built sandcastles. The girls carried water in buckets from the lake's edge to fill the moats that they had dug. When they were completely covered with sand, they would go back in the water to rinse off and get cool.

Shadows were growing along the shore when Strawberry Rose waved goodbye to Buttercup and helped her grandparents carry the beach and picnic things back up to the house.

After dinner, Strawberry Rose had just finished drying the last plate when she heard a pickup truck in the driveway.

Grandma peered out the kitchen window and happily announced, "Rose, a surprise has arrived for you!"

Strawberry Rose, Grandma, and Grandpa went out to meet the surprise guest as he was unloading his old white pickup truck. It was Cousin Jimmy! He wore dusty blue jeans, a dark blue short-sleeved shirt, well-worn boots, and a baseball cap over his light brown hair.

Jimmy was a tall and strong sixteen-year-old. He looked almost the same as when Strawberry Rose saw him last summer when she came to the lake with her parents. It was a short visit, but she remembered him as nice, smart, and funny.

He slung his bag effortlessly over his shoulder as he was first greeted by a tail-wagging Goose. Then, he was hugged by Grandma and Grandpa. Grandpa called him Jimmy, but Grandma called him Bear.

Strawberry Rose didn't know why Grandma had given him that nickname, but she liked it. She thought it was because he was so big and tall. She decided to call him Cousin Bear while they were at the lake together.

Strawberry Rose held back shyly, but

she was all smiles when her cousin asked, "How is our Rosie?"

Cousin Bear explained to Strawberry Rose that he was going to be there the rest of the summer. He planned to help their grandparents with the old orchard and whatever else was needed.

Everyone helped him bring the rest of his things to his room in the lower level under the screened porch. The entrance was outside, and it had a double bed and a small bathroom. Grandpa had hung an old door for the entrance when the lower level was finished. It was painted with the word "Men," and he'd added the words "Wild Animals" below. Grandpa thought that was funny, and so did Strawberry Rose.

Cousin Bear was already at the kitchen counter finishing up his breakfast of eggs, sausage, and toast when Strawberry Rose entered the kitchen.

Cousin Bear grinned and said, "Good morning, Rosie. Come find us by the cherry trees today. The cherries are ready to pick, and we could use your help."

He stood up from the table and waved goodbye. Goose followed him out the kitchen door.

As soon as the dishes were washed and put away, Strawberry Rose grabbed her bucket and headed toward the cherry trees. The forest path had been overgrown, and she had to pick her way through the brush.

Just off the path, Strawberry Rose saw a deer with two small fawns also finding their way through the woods. They stopped to stare at her for a moment, and then they went on their way.

By the time she arrived at the cherry trees, her cousin was high up on a ladder. Grandpa and Cousin Bear had already filled two buckets with cherries. It was a hot day, and there was no breeze. Goose was napping in the shade of the tree.

"Hi, Rosie," Cousin Bear called out. "We're picking the Queen Anne cherries, but over there are pie cherries. They have low branches that you should be able to reach from the ground." He pointed in the direction of some almost shrub-sized trees.

Strawberry Rose started to fill her bucket with the sour, bright red fruit. Grandpa joined her, and he reached for the higher ones.

"The other cherries are sweet and good for eating, but these sour ones make the best pie," Grandpa commented as they picked. He added, "Keep the stems on these, because that way, they'll be easier to pit."

In no time at all, they had picked lots of cherries—both to eat fresh and for making pies.

Over the next few days, they also picked small, dark, sweet cherries for Grandma to make jelly. The house was filled all week with the sweet smells of cherry pie baking and jelly making.

Buttercup came over a few times to watch all the activity. Strawberry Rose showed her how to pit the sour pie cherries by holding the stem in one hand and lightly squeezing the cherry while pulling the stem. The pit would come out staying attached to the stem. There were always big bowls of fresh cherries to snack on while they worked.

Buttercup told Strawberry Rose, "You eat so many cherries, we may have to change your name to Cherry Rose."

Both girls giggled.

Goose looked at them strangely, and they laughed even more.

When they took cherry harvest breaks, the girls went swimming. Goose still barked when they jumped off the dock and watched to make sure their heads came up.

If Strawberry Rose floated in an inner tube past a certain point, Goose would swim after her, grab the attached rope with his mouth, and pull her to shore. Buttercup thought that was hilarious.

When the weather was too windy to swim, the two friends would stay indoors and play card games on the screened porch. One breezy day, Strawberry Rose looked up from her cards and saw something interesting in the middle of the lake. There were hundreds of logs being pulled and pushed by a tugboat.

Buttercup was just about to say, "Go fish!" when Strawberry Rose pointed to the lake.

"Look, a log boom! Grandma told me about those. They're floating the logs from the river to take to the other end of the lake."

Buttercup added, "I remember seeing big piles of logs there."

Strawberry Rose gave a nod in agreement.

Suddenly, they heard shouting, and they both ran to the kitchen.

Cousin Bear was lifting up the big washtub from the corner, and he had already gathered some things in a bag. "Come follow me, quickly! Goose found a skunk."

The girls ran outside following Cousin Bear. Goose was attached to a tree with a rope, and he looked like he didn't understand what all the fuss was about.

Strawberry Rose thought that meant he must like the skunk smell even though it was really powerful and awful. At least there was no sign of the skunk. It had run off after spraying Goose.

Strawberry Rose said, "You silly dog. There are other animals to sniff around here that aren't so much trouble. Stick with the smaller, less smelly ones like rabbits, raccoons, squirrels, or the cute little chipmunks."

Buttercup started giggling, and Strawberry Rose joined in. Cousin Bear just grinned.

Goose looked at the girls as if he was trying to understand. He turned his shaggy head to the side and stared at them. That made Strawberry Rose and Buttercup laugh even harder.

Cousin Bear filled the washtub with water, suds, and a special liquid for skunk smell removal. Strawberry Rose helped get Goose into the tub. They scrubbed and lathered every inch of the dog.

Buttercup watched for a while, but then she had to leave because it was time for her to go back to her aunt's. She said she was sorry to miss the rest of the excitement but would not miss the smell. Strawberry Rose laughed.

Cousin Bear and Strawberry Rose washed and rinsed Goose until he no longer smelled like skunk. For his final rinse, they untied Goose and walked with

him down the path to the beach.

Tired and hot, they all jumped in the water off the end of the dock—still in their clothes.

There was a log tied to the dock that connected to a tall wood piling. It made a sheltered area for the fishing boat and for swimming.

Cousin Bear asked Strawberry Rose, "Have you tried walking the log yet?"

She softly answered she hadn't.

He stepped from the dock to the log, went a few steps, and then fell in the water with a big splash. "I haven't done this for a while. I'll try again."

He swam to the dock, quickly pulled himself up, and walked to the log. This time, Cousin Bear got almost as far as the piling before he fell in.

"Now you try it, Rosie."

She carefully put one foot on the log, then the other, walking slowly, grabbing with her toes and trying to keep her balance. Strawberry Rose made it halfway before she fell into the water.

Goose was watching their attempts from the dock, and then he started walking on the log too. He almost slipped a couple of times, but he made it all the way to the piling. Then he saw a stick in the water and jumped in after it.

"I guess he showed us," Cousin Bear laughed.

Strawberry Rose smiled.

Cousin Bear said, "We need to get back to the house to get dried off and changed for dinner. But first, I'll check to see if there's any mail."

He turned the mailbox and pulled out a small envelope.

"There's only one letter today, Rosie, and it's for you!"

She clutched the white envelope as they started up the hill. The soggy but not so smelly Goose followed.

CHAPTER FOUR

Fire in the Bay

Strawberry Rose was sitting on her top bunk. Goose had already gone outside. He was restless during the night, and she thought the light of the full moon was bothering him. She'd had a hard time sleeping too, but they both finally settled down. Now she could hear Goose shuffling in the bushes below her.

The letter that came the day before had been opened, read over and over, and was sitting on Strawberry Rose's lap. It was from her mother. No one from home was going to be able to join her at her grandparents' house at the lake.

Although her mom and dad used to bring Strawberry Rose for visits when she was younger, this would be the first summer they couldn't come at all. Her mom and dad were busy working long hours and couldn't get time off.

They had made other arrangements to get her home at the end of the summer. Strawberry Rose understood this, but she still felt sad. She didn't know if she felt this way for her or for them. Strawberry Rose reminded herself that she was brave and they all would be fine.

She brushed away her tears and thought again about Goose and last night's full moon. She imagined him howling at it, and that made her giggle.

Outside the screened porch, Goose started to bark loudly and intently. Strawberry Rose looked up and saw smoke. It was rising through the trees close by, maybe at the neighbors'. It was getting thicker.

Strawberry Rose climbed down from her bunk, dropping her letter on the floor, and ran into the kitchen. Her grandparents and Cousin Bear were sitting around the table finishing their coffee.

"Smoke next door!" cried Strawberry Rose in alarm.

Grandpa and Cousin Bear practically flew out of the house and down the path toward the beach. Strawberry Rose ran quickly after them.

Grandma stayed inside but called out as Strawberry Rose raced down the path, "Keep your distance from the fire!"

By the time she reached the lakeshore, Grandpa had pulled a pump and two long hoses out of the beach shed. Cousin Bear hauled one coiled hose, and the pump attached with a second hose, to the neighbors' front yard. Grandpa put the other end of the second hose in the lake and then followed Cousin Bear.

A brush fire had been built too close to an old, dry pine tree and had gotten out of control. The bright, smoky flames were burning the lower branches and were starting to go up the tree. Their neighbor wasn't having any luck putting it out with his garden hose.

Grandpa turned and ordered, "Stay back, Rose. You too, Goose."

Strawberry Rose hadn't noticed that the dog was right behind her. They both stopped and stared at the fire through the trees. Buttercup came running over to join them on the beach and watch.

The fire had gotten very hot. The pine needles were sizzling loudly, and the fire was growing. Strawberry Rose and

Buttercup could hear the roar of the flames. They were both scared and watched in awe as they held tightly onto Goose to keep him safely away.

Cousin Bear started the motor of the pump after uncoiling and attaching the extra hose. The water gushed out, and he pointed it at the base of the tree and the brush pile. After a while, Grandpa took over. They kept spraying water on the fire for what seemed to Strawberry Rose and Buttercup like a very long time. The roar of the fire was slowly replaced by the hiss of a few gray wisps of steam.

It finally died down to a big, soggy mess that smelled wet and smoky. Everyone who had gathered around looked relieved. Goose, still with Strawberry Rose and Buttercup, whined softly.

The neighbor that started the brush fire said to the crowd, "I appreciate the help. I wasn't as careful as I should have been and had no idea the fire could get out of control so quickly. Thank you to everyone who kept this from being a very bad situation." He looked gratefully at Grandpa and Cousin Bear.

All the adults started talking at once. They were so glad that the fire hadn't spread far. Many shook hands with each other, and some patted Grandpa and Cousin Bear on the back. Then they all began to return to their homes.

Buttercup waved to Strawberry Rose as she walked toward her aunt's cabin. Strawberry Rose waved back, and Goose barked a goodbye.

Strawberry Rose relaxed a bit when she saw Grandpa and Cousin Bear returning to the beach to put the pump and the hoses back in the shed. They all walked silently up the hill to the house.

Just before they arrived at the kitchen door, Cousin Bear turned to Strawberry Rose. "Good job spotting that fire, Rosie. You too, Goose."

Grandpa nodded at her in approval, gave her a wink, and then patted the dog on the head.

Strawberry Rose felt proud that she was able to help in some way and was very relieved that the danger was over.

Grandma was washing dishes in a sink of soapy water as they entered the kitchen. Strawberry Rose started describing what had happened, and Grandpa and Cousin Bear joined in.

Grandma reached for the kitchen towel and dried her hands while listening to each account. Then she pointed to an overflowing basket in the corner. "I gathered some things that we'd need if the fire got out of hand and we had to leave quickly. But, thanks to everyone's brave efforts, we're all safe."

Strawberry Rose, Cousin Bear, and Grandpa grinned.

The rest of the day was spent helping Grandma in the kitchen canning fruits and vegetables. Grandpa and Cousin Bear brought in baskets full of tomatoes, corn, peas, green beans, new potatoes, and carrots to be preserved. Plums were starting to ripen, so Cousin Bear also brought in a bucket of the sweet purple fruits.

Strawberry Rose helped her grandmother clean and peel the produce. She also kept up with the piles of dishes.

When they were done, Grandma sent her out with a container to pick strawberries. Grandpa and Cousin Bear were done with what they had planned to harvest that day, but they were still in the garden repairing a section of the fence.

Strawberry Rose quietly went to work, and soon, her bucket was flowing over with strawberries. She carefully held the bucket and walked slowly toward the house so she wouldn't spill.

Buttercup was coming up the path, and this time, she was wearing two daisy chain necklaces. She put one over Strawberry Rose's head and said, "What a wild day—so here are some wildflowers."

Both girls giggled, and together, they brought the bucket of strawberries to the kitchen.

"Perfect," Grandma commented as she admired the berries. "I think everyone is in need of ice cream today, and the strawberries will be a wonderful topping."

Grandma had already put all the ice cream making ingredients on the kitchen counter, and also the ice cream maker. Buttercup and Strawberry Rose helped Grandma mix together the cream, sugar, and vanilla.

They poured the mixture into a

container, put it in the middle of the ice cream maker, and inserted the paddle. Then Grandma showed them how to pack layers of salt and ice around the container before they turned the machine on.

Grandma remarked, "In my day, our ice cream maker wasn't electric. We had to hand crank, and that was a lot of work! But you still have to watch and add to the ice. And if it's freezing too slowly, add more salt."

The girls watched the container turn and let Grandma know if the ice was getting low. When it was finished and the stirring paddle couldn't move anymore, they scooped it into another container with a lid and put it in the freezer to harden.

Buttercup and Strawberry Rose each got to lick a spoon before washing and drying the dishes and the ice cream maker.

"Why don't you stay for dinner, Trudy," Grandma suggested.

Strawberry Rose liked that idea.

Buttercup called her aunt for permission and then accepted the invitation.

The meal included lots of vegetables from the day's garden harvest. Grandpa had an extra helping, and Cousin Bear refilled his plate—twice. For dessert, they feasted on handmade ice cream topped with Strawberry Rose's fresh picked berries.

CHAPTER FIVE

Hike to the Ridge

The morning sun was starting to fill the sleeping porch with light, as it had done all week since the fire. But this time, a sound like the meow of a kitten was what woke Strawberry Rose. It was loud, and it seemed to be coming from high in a tree just on the other side of the screen.

Strawberry Rose sat up and tried to listen closely. There it was again—but this time, she saw motion on a branch. It was a bird. She remembered that her grandmother had told her about a type of bird that sounded like a cat. It was called a catbird, of course. Strawberry Rose laughed and got out of bed.

She put on long pants, a shirt with

long sleeves, and her sturdy shoes. Buttercup and Strawberry Rose were going on a hike up to the ridge overlooking the lake. They had planned to do this when the weather was predicted to be warm but not too hot. Today was the day!

At breakfast, Strawberry Rose saw that Grandma had already made two picnic lunches. She reminded her grandmother that Buttercup was packing her own lunch for the hike.

"This one is for Bear," Grandma explained. "He's going with you to check on some things along the way."

Strawberry Rose was excited. He always made things more interesting, no matter what it was.

By the time Strawberry Rose had helped with the breakfast dishes and cleaned up her sleeping area, Buttercup was at the kitchen door. Cousin Bear was there too.

He had gone out earlier to make walking sticks for the two girls in their size. He had one as well, but it was much taller. Strawberry Rose and Buttercup were all smiles as they admired how pretty and smooth they were.

"I had to go far into the woods to find sticks this straight," noted Cousin

Bear. He looked pleased that they liked them.

The three of them started walking up the hill behind the house. They each had backpacks and their walking sticks. Goose couldn't decide if he should lead or follow, so the dog alternated between both.

The path went through the old, overgrown apple trees, which were all that remained of an orchard planted a long time ago. The apples were small and green and hard to see through the thick leaves.

Cousin Bear stopped every so often to look at the apples. He could name almost every variety, although some were his best guesses because the trees were so old.

It was a constant battle between the trees and the forest for light. Mostly, the tall pine and fir trees won, leaving a dark and leafless apple tree in their shadow. But there were still plenty of trees that were doing well in the struggle. They had found small rays of the sun through the forest canopy.

Cousin Bear explained that he and Grandpa were working with other orchards to grow new trees from some of these very old ones. "We're collecting special cuttings from the old apple trees in the early spring, and we share these with experts to graft into baby trees. By doing this, the rare apples won't be lost."

Strawberry Rose and Buttercup nodded in agreement that this was a very good thing, but they laughed at the words "baby trees."

The sun was rising above some of the trees, so they knew it was now late morning. As they climbed higher, the path opened up to a meadow. There were wildflowers everywhere.

Buttercup put down her pack and walking stick to run through the field. Then she picked a bunch of daisies. There were also small, purple flowers of vetch, orange Indian paintbrush, and white clover.

Strawberry Rose, Buttercup, and Cousin Bear stopped to sip from their water bottles and then continued walking up the hill along the path. Goose started to run after a rabbit, but after a few minutes, he rejoined the hikers on the trail.

At this point, the path was overgrown and not well marked. They had to pick their way through brush and fallen tree limbs. Strawberry Rose was glad she was wearing her sturdy shoes.

Soon, the woods opened up, and it was easier going. The path twisted and turned higher up the hill.

Around the next bend, there were tall grasses, and the ground was soggy. Cousin Bear pointed out the cattail plants with their long, brown flower spikes.

As they walked closer to where the cattails were getting thick, Cousin Bear picked up a rock. He took a few more steps and threw the rock toward the tall, green plants.

Strawberry Rose was surprised to hear a splash.

"That's my favorite spring," Cousin Bear exclaimed.

A few moments later, they heard Goose lapping up water.

"I think it's Goose's favorite spring too," added Strawberry Rose.

They all laughed and continued up toward the ridge.

Just past the spring, Buttercup shouted out, "Raspberries!"

Both she and Strawberry Rose ran toward the large black raspberry plants with spiked stems full of the sweet, dark berries. Strawberry Rose and Buttercup's fingers became covered with purple juice as they ate their fill. They were careful to avoid the thorns.

Strawberry Rose pointed when she spotted something sticking up in the dirt near the black raspberries.

Cousin Bear picked it up. It was a bear skull. All three of them looked in awe at the bleached-white bones.

"This is a reminder for everyone to keep an eye out," warned Cousin Bear. "There aren't any grizzlies in the area, but we do have black bears around here. They pretty much keep to themselves and will try to avoid you, but you sure don't want to surprise them."

Buttercup and Strawberry Rose glanced at each other with wide eyes, as if they were both imagining running into a real live black bear. Then they shook their heads in agreement with Cousin Bear's statement.

Ahead on the trail, Goose began barking. They all ran toward him as quickly and quietly as they could. Cousin Bear arrived first, and the girls were close behind him.

In front of Goose was a large porcupine with its huge quills sticking out all over. Though Goose was barking at it, he was not getting close to the sharp spines.

Cousin Bear grabbed the dog's collar, quickly attached a rope, and calmly pulled Goose backwards. The porcupine, no longer feeling threatened, slowly walked off the trail into the brush.

"I think Goose has finally learned his lesson about those quills," remarked Cousin Bear. "It only took him thirteen times."

"Thirteen times?" Buttercup asked in surprise.

Cousin Bear responded, "Porcupines

are very good at self-defense, and it took Goose a lot of tries to figure that out!"

Buttercup added, "The quills are sharp! They must be painful."

Strawberry Rose heartily agreed. "I'm so glad Goose didn't get hurt this time—or the porcupine!"

They all looked at each other and nodded, relieved and happy that the dog had behaved. However, Goose was kept on the rope close to the hikers until they put a good distance between the dog and the porcupine.

The trail ended at a steep rocky part where Cousin Bear felt it was safe to untie Goose. They all scrambled up the slope to the top of the hill.

Strawberry Rose and Buttercup gasped at the view of the blue lake glistening in the distance. It was surrounded by tall, dark hills and topped by a bright blue sky. They could barely see the boats on the lake below since they were quite far up.

"Everything looks so tiny," noted Strawberry Rose.

"And look at the wakes that the boats make on the water," Buttercup added. "It's all so pretty!"

Cousin Bear pointed and said, "Over

in that direction is the cabin. You can see a small part of the roof through the trees."

They all stood silently and admired the beautiful view for a while longer.

The sun was shining directly overhead now, and there weren't many clouds, so it was starting to get hot. They took shelter in the shade of a large pine tree and ate their packed lunches.

In addition to their water bottles, Grandma had prepared peanut butter sandwiches, sliced cucumbers and carrots, cheese, and plenty of cookies to share. Buttercup's aunt had packed a cheese sandwich, an apple, and brownies for everyone. They ate their fill, and Cousin Bear took care of any leftovers. After resting a bit, they started the long trek home.

Buttercup exclaimed, "The first thing I'm going to do when we get back is jump in the lake!"

Strawberry Rose and Cousin Bear agreed. Even Goose seemed to perk up at the suggestion.

As soon as they got home, they did. They all swam for the rest of the afternoon, and the cool lake water never felt more refreshing.

CHAPTER SIX

The Dust Storm

It was a warm day, and Strawberry Rose decided to go swimming. Buttercup was in town with her aunt for a few days, so she knew not to look for her at the lake.

Goose was happy to follow Strawberry Rose to the dock. He lay down near her towel and chewed on a stick.

Strawberry Rose went swimming and tried walking the log again. This time, she almost got to the end before falling off. She returned to the dock to dry off and warm up in the sunshine.

Cousin Bear and her grandfather were working on the outboard motor on the fishing boat. It was a fourteen-foot shiny aluminum rowboat that had oars in addition to the small motor. Inside, there were two fishing poles, a cooler, a fishing box, life jackets, and a throw cushion.

Grandpa was sitting in the boat near the motor, wearing old faded denim overalls. He was handing tools out of his toolbox to Cousin Bear and giving directions on what to do. He always had a clear and calm voice, even when a part fell into the water and his grandson had to dive for it. It took them a few hours before they were finally finished.

"Good job on replacing the spark plug and everything else," Grandpa proudly said to a soggy Cousin Bear.

The motor was fixed and running smoothly. After they filled the fuel tank from a gasoline container, Grandpa walked up the hill carrying the gas can and his tools.

He whistled for Goose, and the dog ran to join him at the house.

"Hey, Rosie," Cousin Bear called out, "do you want to go fishing?"

"Sure," answered Strawberry Rose, and she pulled her shorts and t-shirt over her now dry swimsuit.

She put on a life jacket, and Cousin Bear helped her adjust the buckles. He put one on over his almost dry t-shirt.

They weren't going out far. The best fishing was across the opening of the bay. They planned to start at the end by the big rock that Strawberry Rose and Buttercup had scrambled over when going to Driftwood Beach.

They would slowly cross the bay using the trolling motor on a very low speed. Then they would turn around and go back again, crossing the bay many times.

They carefully put bait on the silver and red hooks. Cousin Bear pointed out the different parts of the fishing line.

Strawberry Rose thought the names sounded weird and were a little confusing, but she listened as best as she could. There was a combination of the almost invisible but strong fishing leader, rubbery snubbers, bright shining flashers, and multi-colored lead line on the fishing pole reel.

Cousin Bear said that because the line was heavy, the fishing lure with the bait would go down deep into the water. The silver flashers would attract the fish to the bait.

They were after kokanee, a small landlocked salmon. She knew that they were pink on the inside, and she really liked the dinners they had of these fish and fresh corn from the garden.

Cousin Bear explained to Strawberry Rose that these fish didn't travel up the rivers like other salmon. Kokanee stayed in the lake to spawn.

Strawberry Rose held one fishing pole while Cousin Bear had his on the other side of the boat. He was carefully keeping the motor on the correct speed and heading in the right direction.

Cousin Bear laughed when Strawberry Rose said, "Here, fishy, fishy!"

But, minutes later, her fishing pole started to move and bend. With his pole in a holder and the motor on idle, Cousin Bear helped Strawberry Rose reel up the silvery and slippery kokanee. It was putting up a good fight.

When the fish came to the surface, Cousin Bear scooped it up in a net. He smiled. "Good job, Rosie!"

Strawberry Rose beamed.

Cousin Bear landed the next three fish, and Strawberry Rose caught two more. All of the kokanee were placed into the cooler full of ice.

It was starting to get a little late in the afternoon, and they talked about heading back to the dock. Cousin Bear pulled his line up and secured the hook on his fishing pole. Strawberry Rose started to do the same when all of a sudden, the wind picked up.

They both looked in the direction the wind was coming from. In the distance, they saw a big wall of what looked like dirt or dust filling the horizon.

The boat started to tip to the side where the fishing line on Strawberry Rose's fishing pole was still in the water. She looked over the edge nervously, hoping the boat wouldn't capsize.

Cousin Bear didn't hesitate as he pulled out a knife and cut the line. The boat was no longer tipping over, but it was being knocked about by the waves that were now whitecaps. Strawberry Rose was somewhat relieved, although she was still scared of the dust storm that was heading steadily toward them.

"Hang on, Rosie!" he shouted out while heading full throttle toward the dock.

Strawberry Rose held on tightly to the side of the boat. She was frightened and didn't understand everything that was happening, but she knew she needed to do exactly what her cousin said.

"Be brave," Strawberry Rose said to herself under her breath.

The wall of dust was getting closer, and Cousin Bear didn't even try to tie up at the dock. He drove the boat straight onto the beach, jumped out, grabbed the cooler, and lifted Strawberry Rose out of the bow.

"Run!" he yelled.

They both dashed up the hill to the cabin. The kitchen door slammed behind them as the dust storm hit full strength. Both Cousin Bear and Strawberry Rose let out a big sigh of relief.

Grandma, Grandpa, and Goose were already safely inside nervously awaiting their return. All the windows and doors had been closed in preparation for the storm.

Outside, nothing could be seen except dust. The trees, the lake, and the houses were all hidden by a cloud of dirt.

While waiting for the storm to pass, they cleaned the fish and put them in the refrigerator to prepare them for dinner.

That evening while eating fish and corn, they talked about the wild dust storm and how lucky it was they were all safe.

Grandma explained, "These dust storms happen when a storm's wind picks up sand and dirt from the dry fields far beyond the other side of the lake. They come up suddenly, and fortunately, they don't happen very often," she concluded, still sounding a bit shaken up.

Strawberry Rose was still a little shaken up herself, but she was proud she'd acted bravely.

Cousin Bear was a little sad he'd lost a set of lures and flashers, but his grandparents congratulated him on his quick thinking that kept the boat from capsizing.

Grandma and Grandpa were also very happy he'd been able to get Strawberry Rose and himself to shelter so quickly.

Grandpa looked proudly at Cousin Bear and said, "You did well. The next time I'm in town, I'll pick up new fishing gear for you."

Cousin Bear looked relieved and smiled back at Grandpa.

The next day, Strawberry Rose woke to the sound of a downpour. She heard very loud thunder, and seconds later, she saw lightning flashes.

The air temperature was cool, and Strawberry Rose wrapped the wool blanket around her. Goose was not in his usual spot asleep next to the lower bunk, but often, he would wake early to go outside.

Suddenly, there was a bright light and loud crash that scared Strawberry Rose, but she knew that she was safe inside the cabin.

A tall poplar tree on the path to the beach had been struck by a bright white bolt of lightning. Half of it fell, blocking the path with limbs and leaves.

Grandma was heading out to the screened porch at that moment and saw the tree being struck.

Strawberry Rose and Grandma looked at each other in amazement.

"Well, that was something!" Grandma exclaimed. "You all right, dear?"

Strawberry Rose nodded and reached out to hold her grandmother's hand. She had been startled to see something that loud, bright, and unexpected. It was scary.

Grandma held her hand tightly, and it calmed Strawberry Rose. Her grandmother smelled like lilacs, and that calmed her too. It was from the perfume on her dressing table. Strawberry Rose remembered the time Grandma let her dab some on herself.

"At least all this rain will settle the dust," Grandma noted optimistically. "I was looking for Goose—checking to see if he was out here with you. I think he ran off. A thunder and lightning storm really scares the animals."

This worried Strawberry Rose, and Grandma could tell by the look on her face.

Grandma reassured her by saying, "He's done this before, and he will show up once I get his food out."

Strawberry Rose sighed with relief. "Goose has? That's good to know."

Grandma nodded and returned to the kitchen, and Strawberry Rose decided to stay under the warm covers a little longer before she got up to start her day.

It was still chilly as Strawberry Rose sat down in the kitchen to eat. Her grandfather and cousin were still at the table. They were waiting out the storm before going to work around the place. They knew that they would have limbs and fallen branches to clear once the storm was over.

Grandma joined the three of them at the table, and they spent the rest of the morning playing cards. Strawberry Rose thought that it was the best thing ever to do on a rainy day.

She would have thoroughly enjoyed herself if she weren't so concerned about Goose. But, Strawberry Rose knew that he was brave, and she decided she would be too.

CHAPTER SEVEN

Campfire on the Beach

The storm didn't let up until the following day, and Goose still hadn't returned. Everyone went outside and called out for him.

Grandpa and Cousin Bear drove around the area looking and whistling for him, but by midmorning, they returned. There had been no sign of the dog.

Strawberry Rose walked with her grandparents and Cousin Bear to check for Goose in the orchard. They didn't find him, but they saw that the first apples of the season were ripe.

Grandma took a bite out of an apple and declared, "I think that this is my favorite variety."

Cousin Bear added, "You say that about every apple, Grandma."

Grandma laughed and agreed, "Yes, I believe that I do."

The air was crisp after the rain. Strawberry Rose noticed that the sun was quickly drying the leaves of the apple trees. The sky was a bright blue color, and there was a light breeze that was not as strong as the recent big winds.

They decided to pick some apples

and hauled up baskets, boxes, and ladders to the trees. Everyone joined in picking. Even Buttercup, now back from town, came over and helped for a while.

Buttercup asked where Goose was, and was concerned to hear he was nowhere to be found. Everyone was sad knowing he was missing out on chasing apples thrown for him while they picked.

Buttercup offered to help look for the lost dog, but Strawberry Rose told her they'd already searched high and low.

"I hope he comes home soon," Buttercup said. "In the meantime, let's all keep an eye out for him."

After a few hours, Buttercup said goodbye for the day and took a box as big as she could carry back to her aunt's. Grandma, Grandpa, and the two cousins continued picking. Everyone was working away when Cousin Bear stopped and pointed to the edge of the orchard. "Look, Rosie, a moose," he whispered.

A tall moose with large, shovel-shaped antlers was eating apples from the trees near the woods. It had gray fur on its legs, and it looked huge even from where they were standing.

They all remained still, with Cousin Bear close to Strawberry Rose. Moose could be dangerous if surprised. They stayed at a safe distance until the moose was done eating and had slowly walked back into the forest.

Once the baskets and boxes were filled, they brought the containers to the kitchen, and Grandma got busy preserving the fruit. Strawberry Rose helped by taking care of the dishes while Grandpa and Cousin Bear peeled apples.

Soon, there were pies baking in the oven and many hot, shiny jars sealed and filled with applesauce. They froze some apple slices too. Those were mixed with sugar—measured in the right amount—to be used to fill pies in the winter.

The best apples were stored in the cold cellar by the lower level near where Cousin Bear had his bedroom. It was a room cut into the hillside and was lined with concrete blocks. They always had to remember to close the door tightly to keep the cold cellar chilly.

The whole house smelled of apples, cinnamon, sugar, and freshly baked pie. Strawberry Rose thought it was wonderful! They worked in the kitchen the rest of that day and partway though the next.

Goose still had not returned, and Strawberry Rose was very worried. Even though she tried to be strong, she cried softly and had trouble sleeping that night.

The next day was sunny and hot. Having tired themselves out playing in the lake, Strawberry Rose and Buttercup lay on their towels on the dock.

Grandma, Grandpa, and Cousin Bear joined them a little later, and they all relaxed in the sunshine. The only thing missing from this almost perfect day, Strawberry Rose thought, was Goose.

Just before dinnertime, Cousin Bear started picking up driftwood on the beach and piled it in the fire pit. "I think it will be a nice evening for a campfire on the beach," he said.

Strawberry Rose and Buttercup agreed and helped him gather more wood. They set it to the side of the fire pit just outside the ring of rocks around it. They would add this fuel to the fire throughout the evening.

After dinner, Strawberry Rose, Buttercup, and Cousin Bear went back down to the beach. Grandma had given Strawberry Rose a bag with graham crackers, marshmallows, and chocolate bars for s'mores.

Cousin Bear started the fire, and before long, it had a nice, big blaze. The wind was blowing lightly offshore, so the wisps of smoke hung over the darkening water. Small waves that were no more than ripples gently lapped the shore.

The three of them sat around the campfire on logs and used sticks to roast the marshmallows a perfect light brown color. Strawberry Rose and Buttercup were careful not to burn them. Cousin Bear burned two. They placed the toasted and sticky marshmallows on the chocolate and squished them between two half pieces of graham cracker.

Strawberry Rose exclaimed, "This is one of my favorite treats."

Buttercup and Cousin Bear agreed.

Cousin Bear ate three s'mores. Each time, he'd say he wanted some more s'mores, and they would all laugh.

As the fire burned down, they added more wood. Soon though, they let it die down to embers so they could see the sky before the moon came up. They were quiet as they listened to the sounds of the night and the crackling of the fire.

Strawberry Rose stared up from the

soft glow to look at the dark sky full of stars. Buttercup and Cousin Bear looked up too.

Buttercup said, "There are so many stars."

"I never see this many in the city," added Strawberry Rose.

They silently watched the bright, round moon rise over the hills across the lake. It was beautiful.

It was Strawberry Rose's third full moon at the lake this summer. She enjoyed watching the different phases during her time here. When the moon was big and round, the light sparkled like diamonds on the dark lake surface.

Strawberry Rose sighed. She knew that the third full moon meant the seasons were changing. Summer was almost over.

It was getting chilly, so Cousin Bear put a small log on the fire and poked it with a stick. He then began to tell Strawberry Rose and Buttercup what he called a campfire story.

"I'm sure you've heard about the steamship that sank in the bay. I don't know if you knew that it was full of apples and went way down deep to the darkest depths," he began.

The girls looked at each other wide-eyed.

Cousin Bear continued, "This was a commercial apple orchard long ago, way before Grandma and Grandpa purchased the property. The people who owned the orchard sorted and stored the entire apple harvest on that steamship. One night, with no one on board, the steamship mysteriously caught fire. The whole year's crop sank to the lake bottom."

Strawberry Rose and Buttercup gasped in unison.

Cousin Bear paused dramatically.

It was getting really dark, and the girls moved closer to the campfire.

As the fire crackled, shadows from the flames flickered across Cousin Bear's face. "To this day, late at night, each year around apple harvest time during a full moon, washed up along the shore are..."

"What?" Buttercup and Strawberry Rose whispered timidly.

"GHOST APPLES," Cousin Bear uttered in a spooky voice.

Just then, there was splashing at the water's edge, and the girls screamed.

All three of them looked over toward where the sound was coming from, but it was just past the light of the campfire.

They couldn't see anything. They could only hear the water splashing.

Strawberry Rose was scared, but she tried to stay calm. Buttercup grabbed her arm when she noticed her friend was shaking with fear.

A dark shape began coming toward the fire, and Cousin Bear stood up, ready to confront the intruder.

Strawberry Rose held her breath, watching in suspense while the shadowy figure became more visible as it neared the low light of the fire.

It was Goose! The dog was wet and dirty but seemed unharmed.

The girls squealed with delight.

"Goose, we were so worried!" exclaimed Strawberry Rose.

Goose tried to wag his tail because he was so glad to see them, but he was so exhausted, he could barely even wiggle it. They hugged and petted him as they removed some of the sticks and plant burs from his fur. He tiredly licked them gratefully.

They quickly put out the campfire with buckets of water, and Buttercup headed home to her aunt's house. Cousin Bear and Strawberry Rose took a very hungry and tired Goose up the hill.

CHAPTER EIGHT

Summer Is Ending

Strawberry Rose woke up the next morning and was relieved to see Goose still fast asleep in his spot next to the lower bunk bed.

Last night, he was fed, cleaned up, and petted by everyone. Grandma, Grandpa, Cousin Bear, and Strawberry Rose wondered where Goose had been, but they were just glad he'd found his way home. He seemed very happy to be back, and he fell asleep early.

"If only dogs could talk," Grandma had quipped.

Strawberry Rose smiled as she thought about last night's talking dog comment as she jumped out of bed. It was very early, and there wasn't much light as she got dressed. Every day was filled with fun things to do, and she knew that today would be a whirlwind of activity because summer was almost over.

Goose stirred, stood up, and stretched. As if he sensed the excitement, he wagged his tail really fast, almost knocking Strawberry Rose over. He followed her to the kitchen, and they were both surprised that no one else was there. So, Strawberry Rose grabbed a piece of toast from the counter and went outside. Goose was close behind her.

The sky was a deep shade of blue, and the smooth lake glistened. Birds chirped a warning when they saw Strawberry Rose and Goose, and the trees made a rustling sound with their leaves in the light breeze, as if they were glad to see them. The air was cool, clear, and crisp.

Strawberry Rose took a deep breath and could smell the scent of apples mixed with pine as she walked toward the orchard. Goose ran ahead and barked when he found Cousin Bear, Grandma, and Grandpa.

Cousin Bear was high up in a tree on a ladder picking apples. Grandpa was holding the ladder at the base to steady it. Cousin Bear was reaching as far as he could for big, red apples and tossing them to Grandma. She gingerly caught every one, never missing, and then carefully placed the apples in a basket.

Many different varieties of apples were ripe now. Some of them were large, others small, and they were in colorful shades of red, pink, or bright green. There was plenty for everyone to pick, and Strawberry Rose helped until lunchtime.

They carried the overflowing baskets back to the house, and after lunch, Grandpa said, "Thank you, everyone. I'm going to rest then go putter around in the garden. It's slowing down, but there are still some fruits and vegetables to harvest and preserve—or eat fresh." Then he winked at Strawberry Rose.

Grandma nodded and added, "Why doesn't everyone take a well-deserved break?"

Strawberry rose liked the idea and decided she'd go swimming with Buttercup. The lake was starting to cool off a little, and Strawberry Rose noticed the days were getting shorter and the nights colder. This added a little bit of a chill to the water.

Goose stayed very close all afternoon and didn't wander off out of sight of anyone. When he wasn't watching out for the girls while they were playing in the lake, Goose would sit in the shade near the garden while Grandpa worked among his plants. He also joined Cousin Bear in the orchard, hoping for an apple or a stick to be thrown for him to fetch. Later in the afternoon, Goose went inside the cabin and napped at Grandma's feet while she wrote letters.

Strawberry Rose enjoyed a big dinner with her grandparents and cousin that evening. They feasted on what had been picked from the orchards and the garden.

Cousin Bear commented on what a wonderful dinner it was. "Even I'm full!" he joked, and they all laughed.

That night, Strawberry Rose lay in her top bunk in the dark and listened for noises from outside. The water was slowly going back and forth along the lakeshore, and it made a nice lapping sound.

The bullfrog wasn't croaking, and she wondered why it had been a number of nights since she'd last heard him. She thought maybe he'd moved on to somewhere else around the lake. The crickets were loud, but Strawberry Rose liked their chirping sound, and she heard the haunting, lonely howl of coyotes in the distance.

Strawberry Rose looked over the edge of her bed and was happy to see Goose asleep on the floor. He was safe in his spot next to the lower bunk and not out with the coyotes.

She sighed happily and thought what a nice day today had been. She wasn't looking forward to tomorrow, though. Buttercup was leaving her aunt's to go home.

It was late morning, and Strawberry Rose was just looking up at the clock when there was a knock at the kitchen door. Buttercup came in dressed up in a pretty yellow gingham dress with a white sweater and a bow in her hair. She was clutching a small package.

Buttercup said, "I can't stay long because my aunt is waiting in the car in the driveway." She glanced in that direction and added, "I'm so happy that my aunt is flying with me back home. It's so much nicer traveling with someone."

Strawberry Rose nodded. "Are you going directly from here to the airport?"

"Yes," Buttercup replied. "I wanted to say goodbye first, though. It's been a fun summer."

"It has been fun—and WILD," Strawberry Rose added.

Both girls giggled, then Buttercup said, "I brought something special for you." She handed Strawberry Rose the small package that she was holding.

Strawberry Rose carefully opened the paper it was wrapped in. It was a journal.

Buttercup said, "I bought it when I was in town with my aunt earlier this summer. I was hoping you'd like it." She had placed flowers inside some of the pages, which were now dried out.

With a big smile, Strawberry rose opened the journal and gently flipped through the pages.

Buttercup continued, "My aunt showed me how to preserve and press flowers. These will help you remember me."

Strawberry Rose admired the delicate petals and commented, "These are beautiful, especially the daisies." She thanked Buttercup and said, "Of course I will never forget you. Actually, I have something to help you remember me too."

"Ooh, what is it?" Buttercup asked excitedly.

Strawberry Rose walked over to the kitchen table and picked up a sheet of sturdy paper. She had filled it with multi-colored words using her markers. "I made this for you," she replied as she handed the paper to Buttercup.

Each word described something special about their summer. There were words like GOOSE, HIKING, SWIMMING, DRIFTWOOD, SANDCASTLES, LOG BOOM, STRAWBERRIES, DAISIES, GAMES, CARDS, CANOE, CHERRIES, LAKE, ICE CREAM, APPLES, CAMPFIRE, S'MORES, STEAMSHIP, BAY, MAILBOAT, MACARONI SIGN, CREEK, BRIDGE, SKUNK, GARDEN, PICNIC, BLACK RASPBERRIES, ORCHARD, BEAR SKULL, and PORCUPINE. Of course, in the biggest letters of all were the words BUTTERCUP and STRAWBERRY ROSE.

Buttercup clutched the paper and with a big smile exclaimed, "I love this! I will put it on my wall at home and always remember this summer. Thank you!"

Buttercup continued, "I packed my driftwood sign. It barely fit in my suitcase, but I got it in. I'm keeping my walking stick at my aunt's place for next summer."

"I'll keep mine here too," Strawberry Rose agreed. "Before too long, we'll see each other at the lake again."

"That's right. I can't wait!" Buttercup gave her friend a big hug. "Goodbye, Strawberry Rose."

"Goodbye, Buttercup. I guess we'll have to go back to our real names now."

"At least until next summer," agreed Buttercup, and they both giggled. She added, "So, until next summer, Rose!" as she walked toward her aunt's car.

"Later, Trudy!" Rose called out.

She watched the car back out of the driveway and pull onto the main road. Rose felt sad and missed her new friend already. She began thinking of things to do together next summer at the lake.

Cousin Bear came up to Rose and put a hand on her shoulder. "It's always hard when summer is near the end."

Rose nodded.

"I'm also leaving later this afternoon," he told her sadly.

CHAPTER NINE

The Long Drive

Cousin Bear brought his bags up from the room with the "Men, Wild Animals" door and put them in his truck. Everyone was sad he was leaving.

Grandma had packed a big picnic lunch for him, and it included a full-sized apple pie. She also added a box filled with things that she'd canned over the summer—applesauce, tomatoes, and jam.

Grandpa patted him on the back and said, "Thanks for all the help this summer, Jimmy. Drive safe. Be alert and careful."

Cousin Bear turned to Rose and asked, "Do I get a goodbye, Rosie?"

Rose ran over to him and gave him a big bear hug.

Grandma, Grandpa, and Rose waved at the white truck as it slowly traveled down the road. They kept waving until they couldn't see it anymore.

Rose was sad to see yet another friend leave the lake, but she tried not to cry. Grandma gave her a tissue, and she wiped her eyes.

Grandma held Rose's hand, and Grandpa placed his arm around her grandmother. The three of them walked quietly back to the house.

The next day was cool and partly cloudy. It was Rose's last morning at the lake in the top bunk on the screened porch.

Goose yawned and stretched, and then he peered up at Rose. He had a sad look on his face, as if he knew she was leaving too.

Rose scrambled down the ladder and began to pack. She took her things out of the drawers in the dresser next to the bunk bed and stuffed them into her duffel bag. Anything that didn't fit went into her backpack.

Rose made sure that her part of the porch was picked up. She spotted the piece of green glass that she had found on the lakeshore on the Driftwood Beach day. She smiled and put it in her pocket.

Goose perked his ears at the sound of dishes and pans clanging in the kitchen. The smell of bacon and fresh bread filled the air, making Strawberry Rose hungry. Goose, who was hungry too, followed her to the kitchen.

Grandma had made a big meal. There were sausages and bacon on the table. Freshly baked biscuits were in a basket next to butter and strawberry jam. She had made scrambled eggs with shredded cheese sprinkled on top, and there was milk and juice for Rose. Grandma and Grandpa were drinking coffee.

After everyone ate their fill, Rose got up to help with the dishes one last time. Her grandmother asked if she'd rather wash or dry.

Rose answered, "I'll dry."

Before long, the kitchen was clean. Grandma dried her hands on her apron and said, "It's been wonderful spending the summer with you, Rose, and you are such a help to me."

At that moment, Grandpa entered the kitchen to retrieve something from a drawer and added, "A big help to all of us."

Rose smiled and felt proud.

Grandma continued, "I hope you had a good time and you will want to come again."

Goose perked his ears at that, as if he thought Rose coming back for another summer was a good idea.

Rose nodded and told them she'd like that very much. She gave big hugs to Grandma, Grandpa, and Goose.

Goose followed Rose to the sleeping porch where she collected her things. She put on her backpack and grabbed her duffel bag. Goose stayed close to Rose as she took one more look around before heading outside through the kitchen. She opened the door for Grandma, who had her hands full. Then Rose closed the door carefully behind them.

Her grandfather was looking at his truck's engine when Rose and Grandma walked out to the driveway. Grandpa checked the oil, and then he walked around the truck to inspect the tires.

Grandma was holding a picnic lunch for the drive to Rose's home in the city. She put the food on the seat in front. Rose's grandfather placed her duffel and backpack in the back of the truck.

Goose was watching all of this when

he spotted movement in the grass. He sprang toward the spot, and a rabbit jumped out. He chased the rabbit until Rose's grandfather called him back.

"Say goodbye to Rose," Grandpa told Goose.

The dog wagged his tail.

Grandma gave Rose a big hug and told her to have a good trip. She gave her another hug as Rose scrambled into the front seat.

Grandpa slowly drove the truck along the driveway, and Rose could see her grandmother waving until they turned onto the main road. Putting her hand in her pocket, Rose felt the smooth surface of her weathered glass and thought about everything that happened that summer.

On the long drive back to the city, her grandfather didn't say much of anything. At one point, Rose glanced over at him.

Grandpa looked back at her and winked. "On your next visit, I'm going to show you how to change a spark plug."

Rose smiled at him and then turned to stare out the window to enjoy the countryside.

The truck hit a big bump in the road, jolting Rose awake. It took her a minute to realize that she had fallen asleep.

Now fully awake, Rose looked out the window to see where they were. "This is my street!" she said excitedly.

Grandpa smiled and responded, "I'm glad you're done sleeping, sleepyhead, because we're here."

Rising from the front porch chairs, Rose's mother and father started walking toward the truck as Rose and Grandpa were getting out.

Her father was grinning and was wearing a shirt with a tie. Rose thought he must have just come home from work. Her mother was also dressed in her work clothes, wearing a pretty green suit jacket that looked nice with her red hair.

Her parents greeted her with big hugs. Rose noticed that her mother was wearing lilac scented perfume, and she smiled thinking of her grandmother.

When both of her parents said that Rose seemed taller, she stood up even straighter. Her father grabbed the luggage and helped Grandpa carry everything to the front porch, and then the two men sat down to visit.

Rose's mother leaned down to whisper something in her ear.

Rose laughed and said something quietly back to her.

Looking at each other and giggling, they both shouted, "FUNGI MUNGI CHICKEE I O."

Rose thought their canoe greeting was quite fitting for her return home from the lake. She couldn't wait to tell her parents all about her wonderful summer as Strawberry Rose. There were so many stories and memories she wanted to share with them.

Still laughing, Rose and her mother slowly walked toward the house, holding hands.

ABOUT THE AUTHOR

D.D. Glover was born in upstate New York, but she has lived most of her life in the Pacific Northwest. She has a Bachelor of Science degree from the University of Washington.

D.D. currently lives with her musician husband among ancient apple trees on a lake in Idaho. It is the same property where she spent memorable summers with her grandparents as a child. She has three grown sons who, with their families, visit and enjoy the multi-generation tradition.

Strawberry Rose is her third book written for children and was inspired by her summer childhood memories. Her previous children's books *Apple Pie Time* and *Oh no! Where did Monkey go?* were inspired by her children and grandchildren.

When D.D. is not spending time with family and friends, she enjoys knitting, sewing, hiking, gardening, and dancing.

ABOUT THE ILLUSTRATOR

 Signe Berglind Hill was born and raised in the Pacific Northwest. She graduated from Burnley School of Professional Art with a degree in Graphic Art. She also earned a Bachelor of Science in Business Management at Western Governors University.

Between acquiring her degrees, Signe married, raised two boys, and pursued an eclectic mix of interests including quilting, stamping, scrapbooking, and cooking. She has worked as a caterer, craft consultant, elementary school office manager, professional organizer, and freelance graphic artist. Currently, Signe is working for a major video game company, and she enjoys constantly honing her artistic and technical skills.

Printed in the USA
CPSIA information can be obtained
at www.ICGtesting.com
LVHW092116261023
761611LV00001B/2

9 781938 281815